Welcome to A

If you are looking for fast, fun-to-read stories with colorful characters, lots of kid-friendly humor, easy-to-follow action, entertaining story lines, and lively illustrations, then **ALADDIN QUIX** is for you!

But wait, there's more!

If you're also looking for stories with tables of contents; word lists; about-the-book questions; 64, 80, or 96 pages; short chapters; short paragraphs; and large fonts, then **ALADDIN QUIX** is *definitely* for you!

ALADDIN QUIX: The next step between ready to reads and longer, more challenging chapter books, for readers five to eight years old.

Also by Joan Holub and Suzanne Williams

Goddess Girls series
Heroes in Training series
Thunder Girls series
Little Goddess Girls series

School for Magical Monsters series
Book 1: *Rise of Pegasus*

SCHOOL FOR MAGICAL MONSTERS

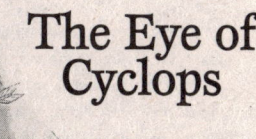

The Eye of Cyclops

JOAN HOLUB & SUZANNE WILLIAMS
ILLUSTRATED BY TOBY ALLEN

ALADDIN QUIX

New York London Toronto Sydney New Delhi

For my grandnieces and grandnephews:
Zealand, Luna, Jackson, Nicholas, Junia, and Sophia
—S. W.

For Andy
—J. H.

ALADDIN QUIX
Simon & Schuster Children's Publishing Division
1230 Avenue of the Americas, New York, New York 10020
First Aladdin QUIX paperback edition October 2024
Text copyright © 2024 by Joan Holub and Suzanne Williams
Illustrations copyright © 2024 by Toby Allen
Also available in an Aladdin QUIX hardcover edition.
All rights reserved, including the right of reproduction in whole or in part in any form.
ALADDIN and the related marks and colophon are trademarks of Simon & Schuster, LLC.
Simon & Schuster: Celebrating 100 Years of Publishing in 2024
For information about special discounts for bulk purchases, please contact
Simon & Schuster Special Sales at 1-866-506-1949 or business@simonandschuster.com.
The Simon & Schuster Speakers Bureau can bring authors to your live event. For more information or to book an event contact the Simon & Schuster Speakers Bureau at 1-866-248-3049 or visit our website at www.simonspeakers.com.
Designed by Tiara Iandiorio
The illustrations for this book were rendered digitally.
The text of this book was set in Archer Medium.
Manufactured in the United States of America 0824 BID
2 4 6 8 10 9 7 5 3 1
Library of Congress Control Number 2023052731
ISBN 9781665917742 (hc)
ISBN 9781665917735 (pbk)
ISBN 9781665917759 (ebook)

Cast of Characters

▧▧▧▧ CREATURES ▧▧▧▧

Cyclops (SI•clops): tall girl with only one eye

Griffin (GRIFF•en): half-eagle, half-lion boy

Hippocampus (hip•uh•KAMP•us): girl horse with a fish tail

Minotaur (MI•no•tohr): boy bull

Pegasus (PEG•uh•suss): boy horse with wings

Sphinx (SFINGKS): girl with a human head, eagle wings, and a lion body

▧▧▧▧ BEASTS ▧▧▧▧

Cerberus (SER•burr•us): three-headed dog boy

Chimera (ky•MEER•uh): girl with a lion head, a goat head, and a dragon head

OTHERS

Arges (AR•jeez): the youngest of Cyclops's three older brothers

Artemis (AR•tuh•miss): black-haired girl goddess, famed in mythology for her archery skills

Brontes (BRON•teez): the oldest of Cyclops's three brothers

Mr. Chiron (KY•rawn): schoolteacher centaur (part man, part horse)

Steropes (stuh•ROH•peez): Cyclops's middle brother

Contents

1

Cyclops Skips School

Hey, you! Yes, you, blurry-looking human reading this book! Did you follow me to this **volcano**? You'd better not tell anyone you saw me here. Or I might EAT you! I'm not joking. (Truthfully, though, I'd rather eat pizza than a human.)

So you've probably noticed I'm a giant girl. Name's **Cyclops**. I go to the School for Magical Monsters. Half the students there are Creatures. The other half are yucky Beasts. I'm a Creature.

I'm bigger and stronger than most of the guys. I can do lots of things better than them. Except for things that need good eyesight. Mine's not great, but that's a secret. Even my brothers don't know about it. Because I don't want anyone to think I'm *weak*!

This morning I faked being sick, though. *Cough-cough. Ha!* When everyone left for classes, I sneaked out and came here.

CLANG! CLANG! That's the sound of hammers striking metal. My older brothers are making armor. So cool. **I love that sound.** It's like music to my ears! I'd rather make armor than go to school any day! I follow the sound toward their workshop deep within the volcano.

It's dark in here. I wish my eye could see better. Yes, *eye*. I just have one. It's big, round, and smack-dab in the middle of my forehead. Cool, right?

I walk on till I see a bright light ahead. Then what does my one big eye spy? My blurry brothers. **All three of 'em!**

When I enter their workshop, a blast of heat hits my face. My brother **Arges** is heating a long metal rod over a huge fire. Smoke rises and disappears through a **vent** in the cave ceiling.

CLANG! CLANG! My other two brothers, **Brontes** and **Steropes**, are hammering armor and weapons. Spears, swords, helmets, and shields line the walls. The bronze and iron ones will go to human soldiers. But the shiny gold and silver ones are for Greek goddesses and gods.

Brontes—my oldest brother— sees me first. He's the biggest of

BRONTES

the three. And, except for a bare spot in the middle that's as big and round as my eye, his chest is also the hairiest! He stops hammering. "Whatcha doing here, Clopsy?" he yells.

Ugh. I hate that babyish nick-name!

Steropes, my middle brother, stops hammering too. "Yeah, why aren't you in school?" he shouts.

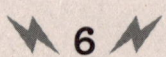

My brothers all speak real loud. Because their hearing's not so good  after years of banging metal. But *their* single eyes see way better than mine.

"Gosh, I'm happy to see you, too," I shout back, feeling let down. I wish they were excited to see me. It's been weeks since I visited. And my brothers are my whole family. Our parents were killed in a battle when I was a baby!

Arges, my youngest (and favorite) brother, pulls his rod from the fire. Its tip glows. He hands it to Brontes to hammer into a spear. *CLANG!* Then he smiles at me and bellows, "Do you bring good news? Did you get your magic power?"

"No," I say, sorry to disappoint him. There are six Creatures and six Beasts at my school. So far only two, **Chimera** and **Pegasus**, have magic powers. Chimera is a Beast with three heads—lion, goat, and dragon ones. All three of her heads got the power to breathe fire. And Pegasus? He's a horse Creature. That guy got wings and can fly now!

Everyone who goes to the School for Magical Monsters will get a magic power sooner or later. But for me it'll be *never*. Because I'm not staying. Why should I? I don't need a power to make armor and weapons. I just need to be big and strong. Which I already am!

I stomp my foot. "I'm sick of school. I want to work here with you!"

Brontes and Steropes burst out laughing, the big meanies. "No way, Clopsy," says Brontes. "You're too young, for one thing."

"Yeah," says Steropes, waving me away. "Shoo! Go back to school!"

Even Arges shrugs. "Sorry, Sis. Brontes is right."

"Please," I beg. "I'll learn more here than at school. **I want to do what you do!**"

"Ha!" snorts Brontes. "It takes strength and skill to do this work."

"Which you'll never have, little girl," Steropes adds meanly.

"I'm plenty strong," I huff. "And I already know a lot." My whole life I've watched my brothers work. I copied what they did with scraps of metal and toy tools that Arges made for me.

"Sorry, Sis," Arges says again. He puts his arm around my shoulders. "I'll walk you out."

"I know the way," I grump. But

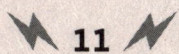

I let him steer me back through the cave. Tears spring into my eye, making things even blurrier than usual. Without Arges guiding me, I'd probably trip and fall on my face!

"Don't feel bad," Arges says when we're outside. "You're lucky to be in school. Brontes, Steropes, and I never got to go." He grins. "That's why we're all such **knuckleheads**."

I don't grin back. He doesn't know it, but my grades at school aren't great. If my brothers are knuckleheads, so am I!

2

Target Practice

I dry my eyes—er, *eye*—and start back to school. On the way, I see a girl. She's shooting wooden arrows at a **target** hanging on a tree.

I squint at the target. One arrow

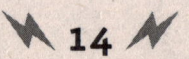

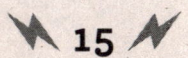

is stuck in its outer edge. The rest are scattered on the ground. **"Oops!"** she says as she misses again.

"You need better arrows!" I

tell her. "And a bow that fits your hand." My brothers could make that stuff for her, but I don't say so.

She jumps around in surprise. "You're right," she agrees. "If I had **equipment** like my twin brother's, I'd be an even better archer than him!" She grins. "Not bragging. I've used his bow and arrows before. With good equipment I shoot straight and true."

I smile. This girl is sure of her abilities. Like I am when it comes to metalwork!

"I'm Cyclops," I say, taking a step closer. I point to my school cap, since my name is written on it.

She points to herself. "**Artemis**."

"I have *three* brothers," I tell her. "They're skilled at metalwork, but I could be too if they'd give me a chance."

Artemis nods. "Brothers are sooo bratty. I hate being told I can't do something. That just makes me want to do it even more!"

Wow! We're a lot alike! I think. "Do you live around here?" I ask.

"No. At the top of **Mount Olympus**," she says.

"But only goddesses and gods live up there!" I say in surprise.

She laughs. "I *am* a goddess."

"Oh! Sorry, I should have guessed!" Sometimes my eyeball can't tell goddesses and gods from humans. Now I'm wondering what kind of magic she can do.

"My water **nymph** friends live in a lake nearby," she tells me, setting down her bow. "About a mile from the volcano. Do you know them?"

"Nuh-uh. My brothers' work-shop is inside that volcano, though," I tell her. "I was just there."

Artemis goes over to take down her target. "I think I've been to it!" she exclaims. "Is one of your brothers named Brontes?"

I nod. "He's the oldest." *And grumpiest,* I almost add.

"I've met him!" Artemis says. "When I was three years old.

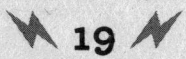

I'd never seen anyone so hairy-chested. I probably didn't think it was real. Anyway, I grabbed a fistful and pulled so hard, I tore some of it out! Mom says she never heard anyone as big and strong as your brother yell so loud."

"So *that's* how Brontes got his bald spot? He always told me he got it in battle!" I can't help laughing.

Artemis laughs too. "I guess it is kind of funny," she says. "So where do you live?"

As we gather her arrows from

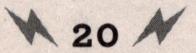

the ground, I tell her about Creature Camp. That's where I live and sleep when I'm not in class. Suddenly I realize it's getting late. Class will end soon.

"Yikes!" I say. "I'd better go! Bye!"

I race back to Creature Camp. I dive under my blanket and pretend to sleep minutes before the other Creatures arrive. Soon I sense all five of them around me. I stretch and pretend to yawn. I open my eye and blink at them.

"Have a good nap?" asks HC. Bubbles float out of her mouth when she talks. Her full name is **Hippocampus**. She looks like a large seahorse.

I nod.

"Feeling better?" Pegasus asks kindly. His awesome magic wings are folded against his sides.

"A little." I pretend to cough.

Minotaur, a bull Creature who stands on two feet, whips out his bullhorn. "Hooray, everyone!" he roars into it. "Cyclops is not gonna die!"

I roll my eye. **"Duh."**

Sphinx, a girl with a human head and a lion's body, is holding some papers in her front paws.

"Guess what I brought you?" she asks. "It rhymes with *foam work*." Riddles are her favorite thing.

"Homework," I reply, frowning. "Thanks for nothing."

Griffin opens his beak and laughs. (He's half eagle and half lion.) "I brought you a snack. Here!" he squawks. He holds out a bag clutched in his claws.

I wrinkle my nose. "Ew! Stinky! What is it?"

"A goldfish head!" Griffin loves anything that's gold, dead or alive.

"Ugh! No, thanks!" I say. I'd
been hoping for pizza. Suddenly I
feel grouchy. "This fish is yucky!"
I snap at poor Griffin. Then I glare
at Sphinx. "And thanks to you,
now I have homework to do!"

I'm being rude, but I can't seem
to stop. "Go away, all of you!" I

yell. Then I pull the covers over my head.

Later I look at the homework. It's a story with questions about a long-ago battle. (*Not* the fake one Brontes told me about!) As usual, the words fuzz together when I try to read them.

After a while I give up. If only my brothers would let me quit school! Would they change their minds if I could prove my metal-working skills?

I think of Artemis. Even without

a good bow and arrows, she believes in her skill. How much do I believe in mine?

Hey! I get an idea. What if I make Artemis all the equipment she needs? That would prove my skill *and* help my new friend. Yes! **I'll do it.** After my brothers leave the volcano tomorrow, I'll sneak in. Their workshop will be mine for the whole night!

3

A New Plan

The next morning before class, I try to sneak a candle into my school bag before leaving Creature Camp. Sphinx and Pegasus catch me. "What's that for?" Pegasus asks.

None of your beeswax! I almost growl. But I stop myself from acting grouchy again. My problems aren't their fault, after all.

"I'm going to my brothers' workshop after school," I admit. I don't tell them my brothers won't be there. "It'll be dark by then, so I'll need the candle to light my way inside the volcano."

"Ooh! That reminds me," says Sphinx as we head to class. "Why is telling jokes to a volcano a bad idea?"

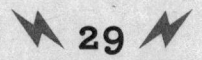

"Don't know. Why?" I reply.

Sphinx grins. "Because it might **erupt** in laughter!"

Pegasus and I groan, but we also laugh.

Soon we reach Mighty Meadow. Our teacher, **Mr. Chiron**, named it that. Because it's where we learn, and learning makes us mighty, he says.

Colorful flags atop poles form a circle around the meadow. I squint and move carefully so I won't bump into one as I walk between

them. Then I sit on the grass.

Soon all twelve students at the School for Magical Monsters have arrived. Beasts live at Beast Base. It looks a lot like Creature Camp, but it's not as cool. Because, duh, yucky Beasts stay there!

"Move over, One-Eye!" a Beast boy with three dog heads growls at me.

I do the math in my head. (3 heads × 2 eyes each = 6 eyes.) Then I growl back, "Sit somewhere else, Six-Eyes!" His real name is **Cerberus**.

He sits down next to me anyway. *Sigh*.

Sphinx is on my other side. "I think Cerberus wants to be friends," she whispers.

I snort. "Funny way of showing it," I whisper back.

Pop! Mr. Chiron magically appears before us. He's a **centaur**, half human and half horse, and can pop himself here, there, or anywhere. "Today we'll learn to make something from metal," he tells us.

My ears perk up. Yes! **This sounds fun!**

"For this project, you'll work in pairs," he goes on.

Sphinx and I smile at each other, but then our teacher says, "One Creature and one Beast per pair."

Argh! Mr. Chiron is always trying to get Creatures and Beasts to get along. Good luck with that!

Cerberus's heads all turn toward

me. "Hey, partner," he says.

You wish, dog breath, I almost say. But then I decide one Beast is as good—or *bad*—as any other. "Fine," I mutter.

Mr. Chiron clicks his boot heels together. Instantly, six toadstool tables—one per student pair—magically appear. I squint at them. Atop each table is a thin sheet of metal and a few other things I can't quite make out.

"Today you and your partner will create a **sculpture** together,"

Mr. Chiron tells us. "It can be whatever you want."

"Pretty lame directions," Cerberus grumbles as we head for a table.

I don't say it, but I'm guessing Mr. Chiron doesn't care about metalwork. He just wants us Creatures and Beasts to mix more and learn to get along.

"No worries," I say. "I've been making things from metal since I was little!"

"Think smart, and be creative,"

Mr. Chiron tells everyone now. "Be your best self, and your special power might find you today!" It's the same thing he tells us *every* day.

"Rrright," Cerberus growls. "I think my special power must be on vacation somewhere far away. Because I'm *always* my best self."

"Really?" I can't help saying to him. "Then I'd hate to see how growly your *worst* self is!"

And to my surprise, Cerberus laughs. **"Good one!"** he says.

I smile a little, pleased I made him laugh. I didn't know he had a sense of humor!

Besides the metal, there are two pairs of scissors, a spool of wire, sandpaper, and two small pointed sticks.

"What should we make?" Cerberus asks.

"A tree, maybe?" I suggest. "I can show you how."

I half expect Cerberus to make fun of my idea. But he just shrugs and says, "Okay."

I show him how to use his pointy stick to press down on the metal sheet. We draw outlines of twenty leaves. Next we cut them out of the thin metal. Then I make veins on the leaves with my pointy stick.

Cerberus tries too, but his lines are uneven. "This is harder than it looks," he says.

"Not for me," I say proudly. Doing something that's easy for me (unlike reading!) feels great. **"Yeah,"** Cerberus agrees. "You're really good at this."

I smile. "Thanks!" Next I show him how to sand the front and back of the leaves to smooth out bumps in the metal. While he does that, I craft a metal tree stand with metal branches.

"Can you make a small hole at the end of each leaf's stem?" I ask once he finishes the sanding.

Cerberus grins, showing very sharp teeth. **"No problem!"** he says. I giggle when he uses those teeth to punch the holes. *Chomp!* After that, we thread wire through each hole and attach the leaves to the branches.

"Wow! Awesome project!" Pegasus says from a nearby table.

"Thanks," Cerberus and I reply, grinning proudly at each other.

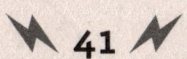

I squint at the strange lump Pegasus and Chimera have made. "What are you guys making? A mountain?"

"It was going to be a statue of Mr. Chiron," Chimera's lion head says.

"But I accidentally breathed fire on it, and it melted," says her dragon head.

"Oh! Too bad," says Cerberus.

"No maa-matter," bleats Chimera's goat head. She and Pegasus look at each other and laugh.

"Yeah," says Pegasus. "This lump thing looks better than our statue did!"

No other project comes close to looking as good as the tree Cerberus and I made. We high-five when Mr. Chiron singles it out for praise. Later, when class is over, the teacher calls to me as I'm leaving. "How're you feeling?"

Why's he asking? I wonder. But then I remember I pretended to be sick yesterday, "B-better," I stutter.

"Great!" he says. "Do you have the homework I sent with Sphinx?"

Uh-oh. "Sphinx must've forgotten to give it to me," I lie. "I'll ask her for it."

"Good. Bring it tomorrow." *Pop!* He disappears.

I start for the volcano. Good thing Mr. Chiron believed me. I feel kind of bad about lying, though. I push the feeling away. If tonight's plan goes well, my brothers are sure to let me quit school and go work with them. Right?

4

Clang!

I hide near the volcano till my brothers head for home. Then I pull the candle from my school bag. It's magical and lights itself instantly.

Once inside the dark workshop,

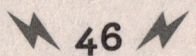

I set the candle on the worktable. I relight the fire and find the supplies and tools I'll need. Then I start cutting, heating, hammering, and shaping.

My brothers don't realize how much I've learned from watching them. Sure, I have eye trouble, and it's hard reading small letters and words. But whatever I've been shown, my hands can copy and make. Even if I have to squint and bend close to my work!

Within a few hours I craft a

beautiful golden bow and three shining golden arrows. I'm very pleased with them! The bow is more powerful than any my brothers have made. In the hands of a skilled archer, it should send

the golden arrows flying straight over great distances.

Time to put out the fire I made. Afterward, I gather the bow and arrows and my school bag. Holding the lit candle, too, I start to leave.

Whack! The bow bumps against the worktable. "Ow! That hurt!" a voice calls out.

Huh? I look at the bow. "Did you just talk?"

"Maybe," it replies.

Startled, I drop the candle.

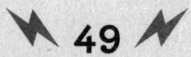

Unfortunately, a bit of lamp oil is on the floor. It catches fire! Flames race across it to a pile of wooden shavings. They catch fire too! In seconds, flames are shooting up the legs of the wooden table. The workshop is burning!

I look around wildly for something to put out the fire. I spy a work apron hanging on a hook. I grab it and toss it over the fire. But it just catches fire too!

Soon flames are everywhere. Smoke billows up and out through the vent in the workshop ceiling.

My heart pounds with fear. Still holding the bow, arrows, and my bag, I race out of the cave. "Help!" I shout. **"Fire!"**

"Phew! I thought I was a goner for sure!" says the bow.

"Us too," three sharp voices chime in. "We thought we were going to melt!"

I stare down at the golden bow and arrows. They all have little faces now, with mouths. "So y-you can all speak?"

"Duh," says the bow.

"Triple duh," say the three arrows.

"But how? I mean, I *made* you! And I can't make things that

speak," I say to them. "Can I?"

"You love your work, and that lends it magic," says the bow. "Should we do anything about that fire, though?"

The fire! I forgot! Outside now, I see smoke and flames leaping out the top of the volcano. **"Help! Fire!"** I cry again. The bow and arrows join in, their little voices worried.

Finally I hear a shout. A deer comes leaping over.

"Is the volcano erupting?" it

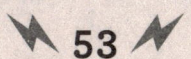

asks. Then, right before my eye, the deer **transforms** into Artemis. Transformation must be one of her magic goddess powers!

5

Artemis and the Water Nymphs

"No, the volcano's not erupting," I tell Artemis. "My brothers' workshop is on fire!" I hold up the bow and arrows. "I was making these for you, and . . ." I stop talking. I don't want to tell her the truth—

that the fire is my fault. If she finds out, maybe she'll think I'm weak and won't want to be my friend!

Artemis's eyes sparkle as she looks at the golden bow and arrows. "You made those for me?" But then she remembers the fire. "We'll bring the water nymphs. They can help put out the fire!"

I shake my head. "But you said they're a mile away. There's no time to go get them and bring them back before the fire destroys everything. If only we could send a message. . . ."

Our eyes fall on the bow and arrows. "Think I can shoot one of these golden arrows far enough to reach the nymphs?" Artemis asks.

"If your aim is true, we'll fly as far as you wish," the three arrows answer.

Artemis stares at them in surprise. "How—?"

I shrug. "Somehow I gave them magic when I made them," I tell her.

"Whoa," says Artemis. "That's sooo cool!" She speaks to one of the arrows. "Go to the water nymphs. Tell them the volcano workshop is on fire and they must bring water." Then she fits the arrow to the golden bow's string. Taking careful aim, she pulls back on the string. It draws back smoothly, just as I hoped it would.

Zzzing! Artemis sends the arrow flying. I cross my fingers that it'll reach its mark.

I give the second arrow a message for my brothers now. "Tell them about the fire and to come right away," I say.

Zzzing! While I point the way, Artemis sends that arrow toward my brothers' home.

Within minutes a tower of

water rises into the sky. Circled by water nymphs, it whooshes over to the volcano. Using their magic, the nymphs send it splashing down through the vent. The fire is out. **Hooray!**

A nymph returns Artemis's golden arrow. "It landed in a tree trunk right next to our lake and gave us your message," she tells us.

"Exactly where I aimed it," Artemis says, proudly stroking the arrow. She turns to me. "Good job making this bow and these

arrows. You've got skills, girl!"

I smile back. "**So do you!** You only needed the right equipment to prove it!"

We thank the nymphs before they fly back to their lake. When Artemis and I are alone again, the golden bow speaks up. "Well, that was exciting!"

"Ha!" I say. "The kind of excitement I could do without!"

Just then my brothers arrive. They do a double take when they notice Artemis and her chatterbox bow and arrows. "We'll be back after we check how much harm the fire did," Arges tells me. All three go inside the volcano.

They're back within minutes. "Totally destroyed," Arges reports sadly.

"Rebuilding will take months," Steropes adds.

"Do you know how it happened, Clopsy?" Brontes asks me.

The arrow I sent must not have told them.

I gulp. I could say that I was on

my way to see them again when I saw the smoke. Maybe they'd believe me. But then I think about all the lies I've told to my friends and my teacher lately. It's hard to keep track of lies. And I don't like how telling them makes me feel.

So I breathe deep and gather my **courage**. "It was my fault," I say. Then I tell them everything. About sneaking into the workshop. About crafting the bow and arrows for Artemis. About dropping the candle that started the fire.

A strange thing happens as I finish speaking. A tiny, round, clear object floats down from the sky. It settles over my eye. Suddenly I can see things I've never seen before! There are freckles on Steropes's face. I see that Brontes's eyebrows

need trimming. And Arges has a small moon-shaped scar on his arm.

An owl hoots in a tree. I look up. I can see every brown-and-black feather! I can even see a ladybug crawling on a leaf above the owl's head. It's like my eye has become a telescope!

"Hey!" I exclaim. "I think I just got my magic power!"

6

An Agreement

Pop! Before I can explain about my sudden super eyesight, Mr. Chiron appears. "Thank goodness you're safe!" he says. "The whole school has been worried about you."

"What? Why?" I ask.

"Pegasus was out flying. He saw flames coming from the volcano," says my teacher. "He told me you'd been planning to head here after school."

Artemis comes over with her bow and two arrows, and everyone meets.

Arges holds the third and last golden arrow out to Artemis. "This must be yours," he says. "It landed in our front door. It told us about the fire and to come quickly."

"Welcome back! We missed you!" the other two arrows squeal to the third one.

"Huh? They talk?" Mr. Chiron asks in surprise.

"Only a truly gifted metalworker could craft a bow and arrows with the power to speak," Brontes says. Then he adds proudly, "Even I can't do that, but it seems that our sister can!"

I smile big at him. Maybe my oldest brother isn't so bad after all. I tell Artemis and my teacher the truth about the fire. Because I already told my brothers, it's a little easier this time.

"Accidents happen," Artemis says.

My brothers and Mr. Chiron all nod.

Phew! I think I had things backward. Maybe secrets and lies only hide weakness. I think telling the truth shows that I'm strong!

My teacher makes a deal with my brothers. In return for teaching metalworking skills to Beasts and Creatures, they can set up a workshop at the school for a while.

"I'll work for you every day after school until the new workshop is built," I tell my brothers. "To help make up for what I did."

Brontes nods. "But only if you can keep up with your schoolwork."

"Excellent plan!" Mr. Chiron says. He eyes my

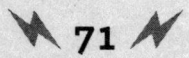

eyeball. "Congratulations on getting your magic power, by the
way. However, I know you weren't
really sick, and you still owe me
some homework."

"Oh, uh, yes, sorry. I'll get it done.
And I'm through with lying. Prom-
ise," I say. Mr. Chiron is known for
being wise, so I guess I should've
figured I couldn't fool him. He even
knew what my new magic power
was before I could tell anyone!

"You'll come work at the school
tomorrow, then?" Mr. Chiron asks

my brothers, raising an eyebrow.

They nod.

To me the teacher says, "See you back at school soon." *Pop!*

"Magic power?" Artemis says after he's gone. "What's that all about?"

I explain about my new super eyesight.

Arges peers at my eye. "It does look clearer and brighter."

A butterfly flutters toward us just then. I describe the color-ful markings on its wings before anyone else can even see it.

"Awesome!" says Artemis. "Can your magic eye do other stuff?"

"Not sure," I say, liking that she called it that. But really, just seeing clearly is magic enough for me.

It's dark by the time I say good-bye to everyone and start back to school. But then I discover something else my magic eye can do. It shines brightly, lighting my way back to Creature Camp!

My friends are ready for bed

when I get there. They crowd around me. I tell them everything that happened. They're amazed by my new eye power. Me too!

"I couldn't see very well before," I admit. "Everything—including *you*—always looked a little blurry and fuzzy around the edges."

"Some of us really *are* fuzzy—or furry, at least!" Pegasus says.

We laugh.

"I'm sorry I've been grumpy lately," I tell my friends. "I don't know what I did to deserve my power. After all, even if it was an accident, I started a fire!"

"Hmm," says HC. "Chimera got *her* power after she carried Pegasus up a mountain."

"And my wing power came just in time to help **Zeus** catch a thunderbolt," says Pegasus. "So maybe you got *your* power because you made a bow and arrows for Artemis—to help her become a better archer."

"Could be," Sphinx says. "But didn't you say your power came right after you found the courage to tell the truth about the fire?"

"That's right," I say. "Maybe I got it because of both those things."

Minotaur whips out his bull-horn. "Woo-hoo! We're in the lead!" he booms. "With Cyclops's new magic power, the score is now Creatures, 2; Beasts, 1!"

Although we all know it's not really a contest, everyone cheers.

My stomach growls. "I haven't eaten since lunch," I say. I look at Pegasus and HC and lick my lips. "I'm hungry enough to eat a horse," I joke. "Maybe *two* horses!"

"Yikes!" says Pegasus. "How about leftover pizza from dinner instead?"

"All right," I say. "But there'd better be a lot of it!"

Later we all settle down to

sleep. If I'd gotten my wish to leave school, I would miss my Creature friends, I realize. Cerberus, too, even if he *is* a Beast! And anyway, I have a feeling my new eye power is going to make reading much easier. Which will make homework and tests easier too. Then I won't be a knucklehead!

I yawn. I wonder what else my magic eye can do? Time will tell. But right now it's time for some shut-eye!

Word List

armor (AR•mer): A strong metal suit worn by soldiers to protect them during battle

centaur (SEN•tohr): A creature who is part man and part horse

courage (KUHR•ihj): Bravery

equipment (ih•KWIP•ment): Things made or used for an activity such as a sport

erupt (ih•RUHPT): Burst out or explode suddenly

knuckleheads (NUH•kuhl•hedz): Foolish people

Mount Olympus (MOWNT oh•LIHM•pus): Tallest mountain in Greece

nymph (NIMF): A maiden who lives in a body of water, a mountain, a tree, or the sky

sculpture (SKUHLP•chur): An object made by carving or molding

target (TAR•giht): An object at which arrows are aimed

transforms (tranz•FORMS):
Changes into something else

vent (VEHNT): An opening that
allows smoke, gas, or liquid to
escape

volcano (vahl•KAY•no): A
mountain or hill that can erupt

Questions

1. What are three things you like about Cyclops?

2. Cyclops doesn't tell others about her poor eyesight because she fears seeming "weak." Have you ever kept something secret because you were worried what others would think if they knew about it? How did keeping that secret make you feel?

3. Why do Cyclops's feelings

about Cerberus become more positive when they work together in class on a metal sculpture?

4. In what ways are Artemis and Cyclops alike?

5. How and why do Cyclops's feelings about her brother Brontes change during the story?

6. Cyclops's magic eye lets her see clearly, even things that are far away. It also shines brightly when it's dark. If

you had a magic eye, what additional powers would you like it to have?

Authors' Note

Hi! We are Joan and Suzanne, two friends who write books together for fun. Our inspiration for the Creatures, Beasts, and other characters in the School for Magical Monsters books comes from Greek mythology.

Cyclops, for example, is named for a race of one-eyed giants. In mythology, Arges, Brontes, and Steropes (Cyclops's brothers in our story) were master blacksmiths. They crafted Zeus's thunderbolts! And according to Greek myth, Artemis really did pull out a fistful of Brontes's chest hair when she was little.

We hope you have fun reading all the School for Magical Monsters books!

—*Joan Holub and Suzanne Williams*